SOS SAG

TRAPPED

Grave Tales

Edited By Jenni Harrison

First published in Great Britain in 2021 by:

 Young**Writers**® ── Est. 1991 ━

Young Writers
Remus House
Coltsfoot Drive
Peterborough
PE2 9BF
Telephone: 01733 890066
Website: www.youngwriters.co.uk

Printed and bound in the UK by BookPrintingUK
Website: www.bookprintinguk.com
YB0460K

FOREWORD

IF YOU FIND YOU'RE GETTING BORED OF READING THE SAME OLD THING ALL THE TIME, YOU'VE COME TO THE RIGHT BOOK. THIS ANTHOLOGY IS HERE TO BREAK YOU OUT OF YOUR READING RUT AND GIVE YOU GRIPPING ADVENTURES, TALES OF SUSPENSE AND IMAGINATIVE WRITING GALORE!

We challenged secondary school students to craft a story in just 100 words. In this third installment of our SOS Sagas, their mission was to write on the theme of 'Trapped'. They were encouraged to think beyond their first instincts and explore deeper into the theme. The result is a variety of styles and genres and, as well as some classic tales of physical entrapment, inside these pages you may find characters trapped in relationships, struggling with mental health issues, or even characters who are the ones doing the trapping.

Here at Young Writers it's our aim to inspire the next generation and instill in them a love of creative writing, and what better way than to see their work in print? The imagination and skill within these pages are proof that we might just be achieving that aim! Well done to each of these fantastic authors.

CONTENTS

Chipping Sodbury School, Chipping Sodbury

Jacob Bowness (13)   1
Leo Salter (12)   2
Rebecca Whittles (11)   3
Daisy Jones (11)   4
Charlie Ray (11)   5
Taya Whiting (13)   6
Emily Clemente (11)   7
Oliver Ball (11)   8

Edinburgh Steiner School, Edinburgh

Nicolas Oggier (13)   9
Isla-May Pearson (12)   10
Katie Zajaczkowska (13)   11
Max Francis Ryczard Katamba (13)   12
Amiya Dhaliwal (14)   13
Magdalena Rohde (13)   14
Eva Cluley (12)   15
Amelka Krzeminska (12)   16
Maura Mitchell (12)   17
Alyssa Macnair (14)   18
Lucy Zajaczkowska (13)   19
Quinn White (14)   20
Ishan Virk-Price (13)   21
Hanna Schad (16)   22

John Smeaton Academy, Leeds

Zack   23
Laila (13)   24
Grace Knowles   25
Brandon Martin (14)   26

Millie-Mae Rowley (12)   27
Jai Riyat (12)   28
Tegan-Elise Woods (13)   29
Lucy Jones   30
Kyra Davy (13)   31
Ellie Wormald (14)   32
Billie Gould (13)   33
Miles Routh (12)   34
Sophie Redmond (12)   35
Kala Morley (13)   36
Theo Allanson (13)   37
Leland (13)   38
Charlie Barnes (13)   39
Matthew Garbutt (13)   40
Demi-Leigh (13)   41
Amber Davy (12)   42
Elizabeth Stanton Stanton (12)   43
Ella   44
Dylan Pickett-Smith (13)   45
Cerys Thomas (13)   46
Megan Kibler (12)   47
Esme Devine   48
Morgan-Jean Ralph (13)   49
Erin Cliff (12)   50
Kyle Mckay-Walton (14)   51
Rebecca Smith (13)   52
Joe Crispin (12)   53
Rhys Greenall (14)   54
Maisie Dixon (11)   55
Ruby Cawood (12)   56
Aimee Field (12)   57
Lucas Brown (13)   58
Mya Coultas (14)   59
Julian   60
Hannah Liversidge   61

Imogen Bartley (13)	62
Harry Wilkinson (12)	63
Callum	64
Alex	65
Bailey Smalley (13)	66
Hannah Smith (14)	67
Jake Cooper (12)	68
Zuzanna Malka (13)	69

Lewis Aneke (12)	99
Eleanor McHale (13)	100
Matilda Clothier (12)	101
Taran Singh Bougan (13)	102
Lucy Connell (13)	103
Charlie Passmore (11)	104

Oasis Academy, Hollinwood

Parul Randev (12)	70

St Edmund's Catholic Academy, Wolverhampton

Natalie Kyei (11)	71
Izedonmwen-Irabor (11)	72
Harriet Deadman (12)	73
Miguel Muhamed (11)	74
Rose Fisher (12)	75
Megan Grove (11)	76
Letty Zollino (13)	77
Lucas Charlie Trainer (12)	78
Zion Ellis-White (11)	79
Holly Portlock (11)	80
Mujtaba Kazmi (13)	81
Kian Bowdler (12)	82
Pavneet Kaur	83
Niamh O'Donnell (11)	84
Lara Hiwa (11)	85
Sarrinah Hussain (12)	86
Emmanuella Addo (12)	87
Rose Mason (12)	88
Panashe Shoniwa (13)	89
Grace Watkiss-Rooney (12)	90
Mohammed Toqir (13)	91
Oskar Zalewczak (11)	92
Evie Neale	93
Mia-Mae McDermott (12)	94
Daniel Francis (12)	95
Chimeremma Agbasoga (13)	96
Eshan Ali (12)	97
Isha Bawal	98

THE STORIES

Help Me

They were watching, they always were. Everywhere I went I was being watched. There wasn't one place where they didn't have eyes. At first it started small like I felt like I was being watched. Then it started getting worse like I was being followed home and things went missing. I would even wake up at night to my house alarm being triggered but when I checked, nothing was there. I got counselling but it didn't help. All they did was prescribe me medicine that didn't help.

Eventually they got me. I'm trapped in a dark room. Help me!

Jacob Bowness (13)
Chipping Sodbury School, Chipping Sodbury

Imprisoned

1,242 days I've been here trapped in my isolated cell, all alone. No one to talk to and nothing to listen to. Possibly, the only one in this disgusting place most people escape on their first day but not me because I'm planning my escape right this minute. Then the alarm went off. "What is happening?" I wondered and all of a sudden gunshots all around, then silence. The cells randomly opened and the alarms turned off. I took a quick glance outside and the whole prison was empty and half of the prison had been knocked down. Freedom!

Leo Salter (12)
Chipping Sodbury School, Chipping Sodbury

Time Travel Disaster

"Only thirty seconds left until we get there," Tom said holding the control panel tight. He adjusted his glasses. Tom was a super mind. He could build anything out of scrap anytime. The time machine beeped.

"Are we nearly there Tom?" I asked. It was a bumpy road in time travel. I felt sick. Everyone was awake and alert although looking shaken and shocked at Tom.

"No, now stop asking. It is not easy building a time machine!"

Suddenly it crashed. We were stuck in time...

Rebecca Whittles (11)
Chipping Sodbury School, Chipping Sodbury

Trapped

Only thirty seconds left on the clock, I needed to get to the surface before my oxygen ran out. I was desperate to get to the surface with only twenty seconds left. My heart was beating fast, hammering in my throat. Fifteen seconds remaining and I wasn't going to make it in time. 10, 9, 8, there was nothing I could do, I'd have to die a watery death. 3, 2, 1, 0...

Sweat pouring down my face, it must have been a ridiculous nightmare and there was nothing I could do about it. Bad dreams always happen.

Daisy Jones (11)
Chipping Sodbury School, Chipping Sodbury

The Loop

Only thirty seconds left until it all resets. The man will appear and kill me. I've played into his trap again. The other attacks hurt from when he killed me with a sledgehammer, another time shot by a gun. Everything will go. He is here with a knife. The door breaks down and he comes in. The knife flies across the room and burrows into my shoulder. He stalks towards me. "There's no way out!" he gloats. He throws another knife at my head. I die.

Charlie Ray (11)
Chipping Sodbury School, Chipping Sodbury

Trapped All Alone

All I can remember is going swimming in the sea and waking up in a dark, cold cave. Rocks had covered the opening of the cave which meant I was trapped! All alone with no food and water with soaking wet clothes. I tried to sit up but my body wouldn't let me move, so I lay there looking up at the dusty ceiling. That's when I saw writing on it. I could only just make out a few letters, but what if it told me the way out? Maybe I wasn't trapped!

Taya Whiting (13)
Chipping Sodbury School, Chipping Sodbury

Ugg The Trapped Slug

Ugg was a slug, he was very imaginative. He had one big massive ambition, it was to go to the moon and ride a bicycle. He didn't own a rocket, so he watched some Sluggy Tube and found out how to make a rocket. He went to Slug and Q to get some supplies. He made a rocket! Hours later he reached the moon but he forgot his bicycle! That was the whole point! Then he hit another problem, he had run out of fuel to get home. He was trapped on the moon!

Emily Clemente (11)
Chipping Sodbury School, Chipping Sodbury

My New House

1,142 days I've been here, in a scary, creaky place. There are always two monsters groaning at me, demanding me to do things: go to bed, do my teeth. I'm helpless in this place. I like the old place better as I actually had a bed, I only have a blanket now and I sleep on the floor. I barely get fed, I'm a very skinny boy. I am lucky if I would even get a small piece of bread! I need to get out. I need help. I am trapped.

Oliver Ball (11)
Chipping Sodbury School, Chipping Sodbury

Trapped

On a winter's day, James woke up to snow covering hills, fields and lakes. His friends wanted to play lake hockey. James hesitated, his friends insisted. He had just scored, when a sudden, chilling crack echoed across the lake. James fell through the ice. The pain was excruciating as the frigid water seeped through his clothing. He was trapped. His head ached, his lungs clenched and everything went black. He woke up with a jolt, relieved it had been a nightmare. He looked outside and saw hills, fields and lakes, covered in snow, and decided to play with his friends.

Nicolas Oggier (13)
Edinburgh Steiner School, Edinburgh

Never-Ending Street

The whole street was a mass of people, noise, sounds and smell. People pushed too close, their voices too loud. I was slowly pushing through the crowd. A passing man's shoulder pushed me backwards into a woman's back. "Sorry," I apologised quickly, then continued pushing through. I didn't know where I was going, but it had to be out of here. I'd never been able to cope with other people, I don't know why. But I had one good friend and an amazing family. I still couldn't see the end of the street, but I'd escape this place, somehow.

Isla-May Pearson (12)
Edinburgh Steiner School, Edinburgh

Trapped In A Painting

A thirteen-year-old girl went to the gallery with her parents. There was one particular painting that caught her eye, a dark graveyard. It looked so real. She stared at it. The frame started dripping. When she turned round, her parents had disappeared. When she looked back it was as if the painting was asking her to touch it. She stretched out her hand, feeling a chill run down her spine. Suddenly a hand came out of the picture, grabbed hold of her hand and pulled her screaming and shouting into the dark, mysterious graveyard. Nobody heard her screams.

Katie Zajaczkowska (13)
Edinburgh Steiner School, Edinburgh

The Abduction

I was woken up by a bang. Startled, I decided to check what it was. It was just Cuddles, my pet dog, eating some spare bacon. I was taking a potion when I saw them. I dropped my glass. I was paralysed with fear. Cuddles began barking like hell. I thought they were just myths. Aliens! Then, a blinding white light shone across my now pale body as I felt myself being levitated. Then, in bright capital words: *GAME OVER*. Enraged, I threw my brand new controller across the room. As the screen cheerfully said in bright words, *PRESS START*.

Max Francis Ryczard Katamba (13)
Edinburgh Steiner School, Edinburgh

No Longer Free

All I can remember is the fresh aroma of stewed apples flowing through from the kitchen. A chorus of thrushes sings for me once again.

In darkness I rest.

Screaming runs through me, but all I get in return is the bitter echoing of silence. I throw myself against the sides of the coffin until the clicking of the lock hits my ears. I am finally free from this cage in which I was imprisoned.

"I am free," I sing to myself.

That was before swallowing the mouthful of gravel. And I then realised that I was no longer free.

Amiya Dhaliwal (14)
Edinburgh Steiner School, Edinburgh

Trapped By Bullies

Hazel was trapped, bullied for years, unhappy. Every day she had to choose a new route home to avoid her bullies, kids just like her but stronger, meaner and bolder. The kind that won't stop until they see suffering in their target's eyes. Enough was enough, Hazel had to fight back. But the more she prepared, the more pity she felt. A bunch of hurt kids hurting her, so she could be as pitiful and resentful as them. She would not allow it, she refused.

Instead, in no time she became friends with them and Hazel was free at last.

Magdalena Rohde (13)
Edinburgh Steiner School, Edinburgh

14

Trapped In My Bedroom

I am awoken by screaming, subtle screaming, but I'm still curious. So I hastily make my way over to my bedroom door. It won't open. Suddenly, I hear heavy breathing in my room. I bang on my door, hoping, wishing, begging it'll open. When a muted sound of footsteps gets louder, I jump into my bed as quick as a flash. I hear the same scream but much, much louder outside my window. I warily walk over, I can hear my heart pulse in my chest. I'm shaking in fear when suddenly, *boom!* That's the story of how I died.

Eva Cluley (12)
Edinburgh Steiner School, Edinburgh

Virtual Reality

Sasha, a fifteen-year-old girl, was bored at home. She decided to use her new virtual reality goggles and play some games. When she was finished she tried to take her goggles off but it was no use. She felt panicked and screamed fearfully for her mother. Her mother soon came but she also couldn't get them off. They drove to the ER and the doctors desperately tried to take them off. Once they did, it had horribly blistered her skin. In the morning her whole face was in pain. The goggles were back and she was stuck in virtual reality.

Amelka Krzeminska (12)
Edinburgh Steiner School, Edinburgh

Trapped In A Lift

"Race you!" A boy runs up the stairs just as his older sister steps into the lift. The stairs always win. The lift is old and slow and is going up to the top floor, where the children live. The lift comes to a stop, but the doors don't open. Fourth floor. She has to get to seven. She pushes the button again. The lift doesn't move. She tries pressing various buttons, but nothing happens. Her brother will have reached the top floor by now. He won't wonder where she is, no one will. She is trapped and nobody knows.

Maura Mitchell (12)
Edinburgh Steiner School, Edinburgh

Thinking It Is Over

I can almost see out of the window, but the ropes are holding me back. The rising fire is getting hotter, the bottom of my shoes slowly melting. The smell is awful, the metal grid floor starting to glow red-hot.
The rings on my hand becoming warmer, burning my skin. But the rope's not very strong. It's untangling, my heart rate rising. I am drenched in sweat, and I can escape, but my shoes have burned away. I am walking on hot metal. I punch out the window and climb up, sitting on the ledge, thinking it is over.

Alyssa Macnair (14)
Edinburgh Steiner School, Edinburgh

The Girl In The Lift

Jamima lives with her parents at flat number 6, Hollow Avenue. The babysitter drops Jamima and her best friend off at the big green flat door at 6pm. They go into the small lift and Jamima presses floor 6. The lift slowly goes up to the floor 4, then the lift shakes, the lights flash and her best friend disappears. Jamima faints from shock. When she slowly wakes up, she opens her green eyes and adjusts to the light. Then she sees on the wall of the lift blood-red handprints and letters that spell 'You are next'.

Lucy Zajaczkowska (13)
Edinburgh Steiner School, Edinburgh

Painted In

Harris was going to paint a roof. He saw that some machinery was rusted. He was also running low on grey paint, so he had to use white instead. The best solution for the rust was to put a second coat of paint on. As he was finishing, Harris realised he was stuck in a corner. He had painted himself in. There wouldn't be enough paint to fix the footprints if he walked out. The paint would take three hours to dry. He decided to wait. Looking out over the buildings, he let the waiting begin.

Quinn White (14)
Edinburgh Steiner School, Edinburgh

The Horror Of It

My eyes flash open, dust settles on my face. I sit up, gasp. My foot is chained to the ground. I can't remember anything, as if I had no life before this moment. I hear, feel, a growl. I start to freak out, screaming and howling. I see a silhouette of a girl. After the girl it grips me around my torso with huge pincers. I fall to the ground, dropped in a pool of blood then into its mouth. I'm alive as the teeth sink into me. I shoot up.

I'm alive in bed. It was all a dream.

Ishan Virk-Price (13)
Edinburgh Steiner School, Edinburgh

Scary Man

The dusk started when I arrived at the forest. I was freezing. Step by step I went along my way through the forest. I started my rep music and Eminem began to sing. After seven minutes I noticed a dark, mysterious shadow behind me. I looked over my shoulder and I saw a man. He was bigger than me and ran faster. He ran straight to me, I was scared and ran in the forest. He came behind me. I did not see anything anymore and sprinted. Suddenly I felt a tough blow and sank to the ground.

Hanna Schad (16)
Edinburgh Steiner School, Edinburgh

Trapped In A Desert

Music boomed in my ears and the crumbling canyons and hills were a blur in the distance. Life is great! Abruptly, the rover came to a halt. Its roaring engine was all I could hear. *Bang!* In one blink of an eye, the car went flying backwards...

Sleep summoned the dark thoughts: explosions, screaming, tears and fear. Struggling, I opened my eyes. Tears of fear streamed down my heartbroken face. My cell was blank and bare, covered with pools of blood. It felt like hours before the malignant man walked from the shadows and bellowed, "Your buyer's here. Now move!"

Zack
John Smeaton Academy, Leeds

Trapped

I can't control myself, my mind is killing me. The doctors don't know what to do. Every day my mind feels like it's going to explode. I'm lying in my hospital bed thinking *why is it always me that has to suffer?* I feel like my mind is trapped and I don't have full control of the way I'm thinking. The medication I was given isn't working, that's why I've ended up in hospital. The doctors are trying to figure out another coping strategy for me. Perhaps therapy, but hopefully they'll think quickly because I can't cope with my mind.

Laila (13)
John Smeaton Academy, Leeds

Society

I'm trapped... in a society of 'perfect' people. In a world of competition, forever comparing and claiming to be better whether its facial features or body image. I feel the need to be like everyone else. No pain, no worries, just perfection. But what is perfection? Tall but not too tall. Skinny but not too skinny. You have to love yourself, but not too much; then you'll be full of yourself. The unrealistic expectations that are brought upon people day in and day out. It's not fair, but it's a reality for many people. I just wish I was perfect...

Grace Knowles
John Smeaton Academy, Leeds

The Paradox

The spell was cast. One minute I was in the real world where everything was normal, the next thing I know I'm in the same place but everything seems off and things out of place. I thought to myself, *how long have I been here?*
A sharp voice said, "Oh, you're awake." I had a million questions running through my mind all at once. The voice came again and said, "You have twenty-four hours to escape this place. If you don't you will suffer a terrible and brutal death."
My heart went faster as I tried to figure my escape.

Brandon Martin (14)
John Smeaton Academy, Leeds

The Graveyard

Silently, the moon hung in the midnight sky. The graveyard was no place for a young girl. The hooting of the owls filled my ears, but I heard a voice. It whispered, "I'm watching you, I'm always around." I froze and looked around. There was nobody around. Then there was a rustle from the buses. It could have been a mouse or something more sinister. Terrified, scared, frightened. The onlooking gravestones didn't help matters as they stood there in the atmosphere. There was another rustle from the bushes. I turned around. It was there.

Millie-Mae Rowley (12)
John Smeaton Academy, Leeds

Taken

Suddenly I'm all alone with the vastness and emptiness of space. I'm lost in this world, cut off from everyone and everything. As I stand on this enormous spaceship, loud clattering bangs behind me. The doors start slamming shut. A strong fear and terror is building deep inside and an overwhelming feeling fills my entire body. An icy shiver runs down my spine when more petrifying and alarming thoughts race through my head. Will I ever be rescued from this ugly nightmare or am I trapped here forever? It's too horrifying to think about...

Jai Riyat (12)
John Smeaton Academy, Leeds

The Traumatic Nightmare

Nightmare. Nightmare it was. The most traumatic thing of my life. Trapped. I was trapped. Surrounded by horrible creatures. The nightmare began to get worse and the pub began to get dark. I had been drugged. The illusions got worse. The demons got scarier. There was just me alone. I was trapped. Why me? The nightmare was getting worse. I was trapped in the corner. The demons were getting inside me. I had cuts and bruises all over. It was a nightmare. A trauma. I was traumatised. It was the worst. No matter how I tried, I couldn't get out...

Tegan-Elise Woods (13)
John Smeaton Academy, Leeds

Controlled

I couldn't move, I was stuck within my own thoughts. I was alone but yet it felt like someone was watching. Flashes suddenly appeared and a dark figure in black overwhelmed my thoughts. It was as if I was paralysed. It was like many days had gone but it was only a few seconds that had passed. I was a completely different person with my original self attempting to break out. Flashbacks of non-existent memories took over. Anxiety fulfilled me, imprisoned inside my own mind. How would I ever get out? Will this control my entire life forever?

Lucy Jones
John Smeaton Academy, Leeds

The Exam Hall

"Good luck Year 11!" Suddenly, from every direction came the turning of pages. Mine remained closed. I just sat there looking at my test blankly. My hands just wouldn't pick up my pen like I told them to. Nor did they turn the first page. I just sat in that blue, plastic chair, paralysed. My mind had taken over my whole body. This cold exam hall was where I should be writing away, telling the examiners everything that I had learnt over the past couple of years. But I just sat, staring at my desk, trapped by pressure and fear.

Kyra Davy (13)
John Smeaton Academy, Leeds

Room

We're all alone in this dark, horrid room. There are only three of us and there are no lights. The room is vast and spacious, you can make an echo. There are no windows, they've all been boarded up with manky decaying pieces of wood. The lights that were once hanging from the patchy ceiling now splattered all over the floor. Glass pieces all over, posing a threat to us. The doors won't open, they're indestructible, which becomes a challenge for us. One of us tries to open one of the doors and hasn't been back since...

Ellie Wormald (14)

John Smeaton Academy, Leeds

Trapped

Only two minutes left until the gate opened. I was so excited. But all of a sudden I couldn't move. A big black shadow crept behind me and gripped his hands over my mouth. I couldn't breathe. I could see the gate opening slowly but I couldn't move. Everyone was acting as if nothing was happening. Another person, dressed in black, walked past holding something suspicious in their hand. My heart started beating quickly. I couldn't handle it. I looked away and before I knew it, all I could see was pitch-black. This was it.

Billie Gould (13)
John Smeaton Academy, Leeds

Game Glitch

I've done it. Finally I had made a headset so I can go in the game, I thought. I wore the headset and was sucked in. "Woah that was weird, my stomach is twisted," I said, stumbling. "Wait, how do I get back?" All that monotony for nothing. I was trapped. Slowly the game glitched and was falling apart, no orifice untouched. I ran for my life, clutching onto dear life. I grabbed the edge, falling off. I clasped a code. It was slowly melting me. I knew I was trapped, so I took the easy way out. I jumped...

Miles Routh (12)
John Smeaton Academy, Leeds

Trapped

I can't open my eyes. It feels like someone has glued them together. I feel anxious, terrified to where I feel I could die at this point. Clenching my fists, I gasp for air. As people say, freedom isn't for everyone. Sometimes I am stuck in my emotions. I feel helpless. I can't do anything. I come to a conclusion that I'm trapped and can't get out. I can see lights flickering before me. I keep wondering what my family would do without me if I don't make it. The emotions make me feel abandoned, worried, stressed.

Sophie Redmond (12)
John Smeaton Academy, Leeds

The Forbidden Nightmare

Lost. I couldn't move... There was no way for me to move. There was no movement, I couldn't see, my legs started to twitch, my eyesight started to reappear. Huh? A hospital? I had no idea where I am or even who I am for that matter. I walked along the different hospital wards. Enclosed. A little girl standing and screeching silently. She seemed as if she was dead or hurt. As I walked towards the little girl the walls were covered with blood. "We are watching, we always are." It was like I was gone from reality. Gone.

Kala Morley (13)
John Smeaton Academy, Leeds

It Follows

Everywhere I go, I see that face. It's the same routine every single day. Wake up. Worship it. I want to leave. They won't let me. The large, blinding gold statue of it fills the main room of our praying area. My monotonous routine won't stop. Never. I would run away if I could. It always catches up though. It isn't normal. It isn't human. It makes us pray so we're safe. I wish it didn't have to come here. My monotonous routine begins again for the final time. I'll make it out today, one way or another.

Theo Allanson (13)
John Smeaton Academy, Leeds

Lockdown

It's been six days. I'm trapped here. The sound of his boots crashing against the floor faded to silence roaming through the factory. I have to escape. I try breaking down the cage's door but to no avail. The cold metal talon of a pickaxe rips through my shoulder. Upon looking up I see his gas-masked face. I fall to the ground trembling in agonised fear as blood begins seeping from my clawed shoulder, until suddenly the lights run to darkness. My sight is lost as the sound of metal clinking draws nearer. This is the end.

Leland (13)
John Smeaton Academy, Leeds

The Cage

The cold sun brought no light and the phantom stars fell one by one. The thorns tumbled out of the bushes and scattered themselves poorly on the ground. The trees, tall but lifeless, lingered around the field. The water rushed through the river, a murky purple, but with it came no sound. This place felt like home now after coming here so often. As it always did, the creature lumbered over, its huge arms looming over the rest of it. As my heart throbbed, sweat poured down my face. My vision blurred, all I thought of was the cage...

Charlie Barnes (13)
John Smeaton Academy, Leeds

Trapped With The Souls

It was Friday 30th October 1984, the eve of Halloween. Myself and my brother James were asked to go on a paranormal investigation. I heard the address and felt shivers down my spine. As we approached the double doors I shouted, "Help!" but there was no reply. After what felt like a lifetime the doors creaked open. There was a mysterious, eerie feeling as we entered and all of a sudden the doors slammed behind us. We were trapped. All was had was each other and a video camera to document what was about to happen next...

Matthew Garbutt (13)
John Smeaton Academy, Leeds

Voices Shh!

It's stuck. I can't get this voice out of my head. It keeps telling me to do different things. This voice is making me go mad. Some days I feel like I need to go to sleep and never wake up. I make bad decisions sometimes because I listen to this evil voice that whispers in my ear. I wish I could just pull it out. It's been nearly a year since this voice appeared. I've spoken to people and it's not helping. Argh! I'm going crazy. Help! Get this voice out. It's trapped inside of me isn't it? Help!

Demi-Leigh (13)
John Smeaton Academy, Leeds

Necrophobic

My stertorous breath repelled in my face and my struggles grew pointless. There was no use trying. Doomed to rot in this box for eternity. As I gasped for air, I realised the severity of my situation. There were no means of escape... anywhere. The air surrounding me grew thinner and thinner and the more I tried to scream for help, the harder it got. I was spiralling into pure insanity as the woeful whispers of the dead rang like church bells in my ears. I gave up trying. I clenched my teeth and slowly began to accept my fate.

Amber Davy (12)
John Smeaton Academy, Leeds

Lights. Darkness. Lights.

Lights. Darkness. Lights. I woke up in a frenzy. I tried to move my neck but nothing would move. What had happened to me? My dad was gone. Gone where? The pain was unreal - it was tormenting me. I saw the paramedics grab me. I just couldn't feel it. I was traumatised - was this the end for me? Torches. Paramedics everywhere shining torches in my eyes, asking if I was okay. I couldn't answer. Then I realised. It hit me, harder than my pain. They thought I was dead... My mind went blank. Wait, I think this is the end...

Elizabeth Stanton Stanton (12)
John Smeaton Academy, Leeds

Trapped

The lift stopped. *Darn it*, I thought to myself. The bomb would go off in roughly ten minutes. There was a low chance I'd make it out alive. In my job I come across many dangerous and near-death situations, but this is the closest I've been to death. My heart was racing. I could smell smoke. I looked up and there was a trail of fire on the ceiling. Five minutes. Five minutes until I'd die. I dropped the bomb on the floor. I gave up hope. The trail of blazing fire had reached me. Death himself had arrived.

Ella
John Smeaton Academy, Leeds

The Dark Forest

It was a stormy night. Trees were everywhere in the same sizes. Then out of the trees came a small person. This person was running from something. He passed trees left and right and he didn't bother to look where he was heading. Everywhere there was rain and darkness. He stopped suddenly and stood there, letting the rain drip down his pale face. He then looked at his surroundings. He sank to his knees on the cold, muddy ground. He stared up to the grey sky and screamed, for he realised he was trapped in his own mind.

Dylan Pickett-Smith (13)
John Smeaton Academy, Leeds

The Nightmare

1,142 days I'd been here. Waiting to be free. Trapped in my own nightmare. Protecting my body from evil and saving my soul from spirits. Oh no. He's here. The one I have been running from for what feels like my whole life. My heart, beating like a drum. I hide in the cupboard, my sweating palms holding my mouth shut, trying my best not to scream. I just knew that death was coming my way. The cupboard opened, crashing against the wall. I opened my eyes, hoping to be back to reality. But no, I am still trapped.

Cerys Thomas (13)
John Smeaton Academy, Leeds

Locked In A Trap

22:37. Darkness isn't everyone's choice, but it's mine. I put my head back on my pillow and close my eyes. I can see them, clowns! They keep getting closer and closer as I back up. They have a bright red nose, bright blue eyes. Blood is rolling down their face. They have bright orange curly hair. They are wearing long red shoes with bright blue socks. Their outfit is white and pink. They are so tall. I turn around and more are behind me. Some are short and some are tall. More keep coming. Someone help me!

Megan Kibler (12)
John Smeaton Academy, Leeds

Paralysed

A whirlwind of panic and hysteria is spinning inside of me and I want to scream and cry, but all I can do is lie motionless. My own body is imprisoning me. My panic feels like worms crawling through my veins, squirming through my lungs. My arms feel like bricks, my legs feel like iron. Everything is heavy. I lie like a doll but my heart feels like it's about to burst. I'm trapped inside my shell of a body, scraping at my skull for freedom. Do I look dead? Will I die? My lungs won't move. I feel slow...

Esme Devine
John Smeaton Academy, Leeds

The Trapped Relationship

Another day passes by. I'm still with Noah but I'm sick of having the same arguments. Sometimes I just wish I could leave him. But it's hard. I tried before, he called me stupid and hit me. He cheats all the time. When I tried getting rid of him I couldn't because I was so scared. He scares me. He hits me even if I don't do anything wrong. I have no idea what I did to deserve this. My life could be so much better. Noah says sometimes he doesn't like me. I don't care if he doesn't.

Morgan-Jean Ralph (13)
John Smeaton Academy, Leeds

Living A Nightmare

All I could hear was shouting. Slowly the room started to go quiet. For a split second everything was black, then the bright peeking sun gleamed down. A loud noise came echoing through the streets, then I realised I was reliving the crash. As I followed the ambulance I saw a group of people staring at my lifeless body. I looked up and saw my mum cradling me.

A while later I was at the hospital listening to the doctors talk about me until I realised... I was dead. I was speechless. I realised I was trapped.

Erin Cliff (12)
John Smeaton Academy, Leeds

Trapped

I remember that first night, surrounded with darkness and overwhelmed with fear and pain. Not knowing if I was dreaming or dying or whether it was just happening me or everyone else. I couldn't move, perplexed and encompassed in darkness, just waiting for unpreventable discomfort and misery. Without the slightest insight of what is happening or when and how it'll end. I've been in this state for an undetermined amount of time, could be months, years, decades or a week. I guess I'll never know.

Kyle Mckay-Walton (14)
John Smeaton Academy, Leeds

All Alone

My eyes fluttered open and the pain in my head was the only thing that brought me back to me, thinking *where am I?* My head felt like my brain was dancing. It felt like I had been here for years, but I glanced at my watch, hoping I could see the time despite the shattered glass. I had no hope. I wanted to die instead of being alone. My eyes filled with tears and I was thumping the wall, hoping my escape could happen. My hands were trying to recognise where I was, then I felt dirt falling off...

Rebecca Smith (13)
John Smeaton Academy, Leeds

The Dungeon

I woke up to rusty bars all around me. I was cold and the room was dark. There was whispering around me. As I was trying to find a way out I heard a voice whisper, "We are watching, we always will be." Chills ran down my back and I started to panic more, but all of a sudden the lights flickered and turned on... For a second I thought I recognised the voice from somewhere, it was deep and croaky. I called out, "Why am I here?" I didn't get a reply. I came to a stop and sighed...

Joe Crispin (12)
John Smeaton Academy, Leeds

My Forgotten End

They wait, they always wait. The things that chased me up to the eleventh floor will never leave. Trapped. I am trapped in this four by four room I have escaped to. My food is low and the water bottle is almost empty. Will I survive? Will anyone find me? The darkness of this room swallows me like a wave. My sanity blows away like smoke in the wind and my hope lowers every breath I take. The zombie apocalypse that has only just begun will be the final thought in my head. This is my forgotten end.

Rhys Greenall (14)

John Smeaton Academy, Leeds

Lost And Trapped

Alone and lost, walking in the woods, a cage dropped over me. Then for some reason *pow!* I was in a small, damp room with just a small window and shelves with bullets and powder. I didn't know where I was. I was scared but hopeful. I was really worried and scared that I would never see anyone again and I was scared because I'm really claustrophobic and was in a small damp room with only shelves, powder and bullets, also a small window to breathe. I had to get out of here fast!

Maisie Dixon (11)
John Smeaton Academy, Leeds

Drained

I was walking down the street. I heard a mumbling giggle down the drain. I was confused. I decided to look down and saw a doll's head slowly rise up to the hole. It was horrific, just thinking of how it moved made a constant hill in my body. The sun was just starting to rise and then I heard a voice. "Well hello there! I see you have come to my presence!" I ran and I felt my entire body being sucked out. It felt like I was joining the underworld. Was this the end of my journey?

Ruby Cawood (12)
John Smeaton Academy, Leeds

Fear Of The World

Alone! It still haunts me to this day. The day it all changed. The day that monster took her away. That one day me, aged eight, and my mum arrived home and he was there. My horrible drunk stepdad with an evil grin smeared on his face. He then killed my mum. I was put into care until I was sixteen and every day I was there was just as bad as the day before. Every morning I would dread getting out of bed and the night brought the flashbacks, filling my head with the fear of the world. Alone!

Aimee Field (12)
John Smeaton Academy, Leeds

Nightmare

The lights flickered off. The lift jolted. It came to a stop. My nightmare came true. My whole body froze in fear. The thought of us hanging by a few wires. The woman to my right was breathing heavily. The man to my left was trying to calm us down. Me? I was having a breakdown. I was lying on the floor of a metal box stuck in a building. The lights then appeared. I was filled with happiness. The lift dropped, then it started to rise to the next floor and the doors opened. I was free!

Lucas Brown (13)
John Smeaton Academy, Leeds

Circles

1,142 days I'd been here. It's never going to end. Trapped. I was stuck here. It was a circle, I'd been going round in circles for the past three years. I'd been running day and night trying to find a way out. Every second I was wincing in pain because of running all the time. I was always alone. Nobody was trying to help me. All my life was, was circles. But one day everything changed. I couldn't move, as much as I tried my body was not moving. I was paralysed.

Mya Coultas (14)
John Smeaton Academy, Leeds

All Alone

As the sky turned grey, I walked into the dark, not knowing a black figure was behind me. Then, I got hit. I was in a thick steel cage, not knowing where I was. That very moment, the black figure came back. I was handcuffed and couldn't get out, but then he went away.

I struggled in fear, knowing that if I got the handcuffs off I would be free. Two minutes later, I looked around and found a stick. Then I tried to unlock it with the stick and it worked. I ran home and ate.

Julian

John Smeaton Academy, Leeds

Lonely

I woke up to the sound of banging along the corridors. My bloodshot eyes darted around the crisp, cold room. The wind came running through the window like a ghost flying through to spy upon me. I could feel my heart pounding through my chest. My shaking hands cold to the touch. Two small candles danced about the room, standing furiously on a chest of drawers. How did I get here? Suddenly, whispers began to shout in my spinning head. Shaking, I ran to the door and... I was trapped.

Hannah Liversidge
John Smeaton Academy, Leeds

Trapped And Scared

I couldn't move. I felt claustrophobic. I hated it. I was terrified. I felt like I was in a nightmare. I was in a haunted house and someone had kidnapped me. I was so scared, I heard all these strange and scary noises. I tried to escape but he kept on catching me. I thought I was going to die. I tried to escape again at 10:40pm. I was upset so I did it. I kept running and running until I couldn't run any more. He was behind me. I saw a window so I jumped.

Imogen Bartley (13)
John Smeaton Academy, Leeds

The Glass

As I woke with a feeling of being nauseous and perplexed as I stood on the wooden floor. As I looked around I could see forests and lakes. Whilst the dark clouds departed from the sky I started to wonder where I was, then I began to feel parched so I went to the lake, but I hit something like an invisible barrier like glass. A fear came over me. Panicked, claustrophobic and paranoid. I didn't know what to do now. I knew I was trapped.

Harry Wilkinson (12)
John Smeaton Academy, Leeds

The Kidnapper Story

The kidnapper who lives in a haunted house kidnapped a rich man. He put him in a dark abandoned room. The victim was scared and spooked out. The hairs on the back of his neck stood up. Then the victim's friend beat up and defeated the rude horrid kidnapper and the victim and his friend were free from the horrible kidnapper. The kidnapper was arrested and everyone lived a good happy life, nobody got kidnapped ever again.

Callum
John Smeaton Academy, Leeds

Shadows

Shadows blanketed over me, darkness painting every orifice. Suffocating me in endless fear, it's like I'm being swallowed by the terror of living. Trapped in the paralysis of the mind, my thoughts vanished into the lifeless air. The monotony of lying still for what seemed to be days. Growing restless. Walls forming by my side, a black hole sucking all hope from my soul. Trapped in the endless loop called Hell.

Alex
John Smeaton Academy, Leeds

Left To Die In The Future

I was all alone in that dark empty room. There was a door. There were also cameras focused on me and an intercom. Every now and then there was a voice telling me what was going on in the world in 2941. I never knew why, all that I knew was that I've been in here a long time. I was waiting for them to show themselves and walk in. Stop hiding in the shadows. I was beginning to wonder if... if I was trapped.

Bailey Smalley (13)
John Smeaton Academy, Leeds

Falling!

Help! I was taking the lift to the next floor of the prison but the prisoners had other ideas. I walked into the lift and the door slammed shut. The lights went off and I started to feel as if I was falling. I was falling! I screamed. "Help!" But only heard laughter. Prisoners were shouting, "Bye!" and laughing. I found the emergency button. I... I was scared. "Help!" I screamed.

Hannah Smith (14)
John Smeaton Academy, Leeds

Trapped

I couldn't move out of my chair. A chill went down my spine as I heard shots being fired at innocent people. We locked the door and rang the police. Minutes late we heard sirens and a helicopter so we all snuck out the school by crouching through the corridors. As we were running, my friend got shot but he survived. What a terrifying moment, trapped in that room for what felt like ages.

Jake Cooper (12)
John Smeaton Academy, Leeds

Trapped

My heart starts pounding out of my chest. I put my hand on my chest trying to calm myself down. My head starts spinning, my breathing is short. I am scared. The walls feel like they are caving in. I try to scream but no noise comes out. I try to open the door but it is no use. I close my eyes. No use. I am trapped.

Zuzanna Malka (13)

John Smeaton Academy, Leeds

Untitled

Running late for classes last week I got caught in a bizarre situation. I needed to reach my classes early that day but somehow I got late and in a hurry. I took the elevator to reach the basement. As I am claustrophobic I usually go by stairs, and that day was just horrible. Suddenly the electricity supply cut off and I got trapped in that confined place. Never had I ever felt so helpless in my life. But somehow after thirty minutes the watchman got me out. Since that day onwards I've decided to never take the elevator again.

Parul Randev (12)
Oasis Academy, Hollinwood

The Ceremony

Their eyes examined me. I trembled. Hesitantly, I mumbled to myself, "You didn't know, be content." Suddenly I felt my stomach reluctantly turning. Spiralling into seething anger, I'd forgotten they were still inspecting me.

Exhausted, they bounded towards me, their robes slung around their shoulders like a tarp on a bike. Surely having rituals isn't their addiction? Everything I've known snatched away from me. Tears caressed my cheeks. Sprinting, I became aware making it out alive was my main priority. Remorseless, the members tied me up. My hair tips were partially dipped in the poisonous acid. Blood rushing - *Splash.*

Natalie Kyei (11)
St Edmund's Catholic Academy, Wolverhampton

Trapped

In the dark, I stood secluded. Suddenly, I felt a hand. Evil itself touched me, the horror began gnawing slowly, travelling up steadily whilst I was paralysed in fear. The shadow stood motionlessly. "Haha!" I laughed sarcastically. I was dreaming. The shadow came closer, enough so I could feel its cold breath on my neck. I was in fear, maybe disbelief, but at least one of us was happy. The dark shadow smiled...

"She's awake!" nurses yelled.

I sighed in relief, "It was a dream."

"Or was it?" a mysterious yet familiar silhouette replied, pulling me harshly into the darkness.

Izedonmwen-Irabor (11)

St Edmund's Catholic Academy, Wolverhampton

Trapped In My Mind

The noise of the creaking door echoed around the room. "Hello sweetie," my mother said. "You look lovely as usual." Every time I hear her upset, anxious voice I think back to that day.

One minute everything was normal, the next, horror. I remember gripping Dad's hand and being crushed like a foil ball. For these past two unbearable years, I've been paralysed physically but internally I'm clinging onto life. I can hear everything. The door opens again. "Mrs Mansfield?" a deep voice said. "We have some unfortunate news. After two years, we think it's time to let Lucy go."

Harriet Deadman (12)

St Edmund's Catholic Academy, Wolverhampton

Trapped

Scream after scream after scream. A joyous school had become hell as careful loud footsteps came towards my class. I prepared myself for a long-lasting nightmare then silence. Suddenly, it had seemed that the horror that haunted this school, taking people's lives one by one, had finally left, or so we thought. A big thud shook the ground. For a moment our short-lived celebration seemed like it was over but nothing happened. Finally free, until *bang!* Everything came crumbling down to smithereens before my very eyes, but this is only the beginning of this nail-biting story...

Miguel Muhamed (11)

St Edmund's Catholic Academy, Wolverhampton

Screams

They say screams add to the experience: they're wrong. They say tears make it flavourful: they're wrong. They say the voices in our heads make it more fun: they're wrong. They're coming back. I wipe my tears and try to hide in the cellar that surrounds me. "Come out Clair, we need your help." They say this every time. They tell me it's spreading, if you catch it you die, that's nobody's coming outside. Two men grab me and a needle cuts deep into my wrist like their words.

Blood for the sick patients, death for poor little abducted me.

Rose Fisher (12)
St Edmund's Catholic Academy, Wolverhampton

Sucked In

Air pulled at her, drawing her closer to what seemed like an open mouth with sharp jagged teeth. The silhouetted trees danced with the force. The mouth slammed shut behind her, then she realised she'd been sucked in.

2,834 days later she is still confined in the cage she was imprisoned within. The day the young girl got sucked into a musty-scented forest with the darkened trees. Shuddering at the memory, she continued to try and pick the lock of her miniature cage where she couldn't find any source of light, night or day. She was still terrified.

Megan Grove (11)
St Edmund's Catholic Academy, Wolverhampton

The Nightmare Disaster

There I was, unable to move a muscle. Paralysed. Complete silence invaded my body until all that was left was fear within me. As I lay there still, a faint voice inside my head spoke the words, "You can't leave. Try and try but you can't leave." The voice stayed in my head, I couldn't control the power over me. I waited and waited until suddenly, I heard it. My mother's voice rang in my ears for days. I couldn't forget it.

Years passed, waiting to be released from this misery. I then felt it. My mother's hand touched mine.

Letty Zollino (13)
St Edmund's Catholic Academy, Wolverhampton

Trapped

Heart thumping rapidly. Stiff like a stone statue. All I could hear was whispering and scuffling beside my bed. Just staring into the endless darkness, with the only thing in my body that worked. All of a sudden, the scuffling and the whispering stopped and then something that looked like bright red eyes appeared. The deep disturbing voice whispered, "I am coming." I tried screaming for help, but it was useless. I was stuck in an endless loop of fear. The lava-red eyes then got closer and closer until it was standing at the foot of my bed. Trapped!

Lucas Charlie Trainer (12)
St Edmund's Catholic Academy, Wolverhampton

No Time

The streets of Greendale, being as daunting and suspicious as I remember, suddenly didn't seem the same. I peered over my shoulder and there stood a black, smoky, demon-like figure approaching me at a steady pace.

My legs deflated. My body felt like it was going into self-destruction. A whistle noise immediately rang in my ear like an alarm. In my head, I was saying to myself *who is he?* and *what are they going to do with me?* I hurtled until my house was visible. I fumbled for my keys but I was too late. "Please, no!"

Zion Ellis-White (11)
St Edmund's Catholic Academy, Wolverhampton

Trapped

Trapped. Not mentally trapped, actually trapped. I've been tracking the days until a few nights ago when they changed the wood walls, easy to carve, into noise-cancelling foam and now I have lost track. The last day I recorded was day 545. All I can hear is my heart thumping against my chest and my raspy breathing. They come every night at precisely 12am wanting to take blood for 'research', when I know full well they are using it for the apocalypse they're about to release. I know they won't release me because I know too much.

Holly Portlock (11)
St Edmund's Catholic Academy, Wolverhampton

Lost In My Mind

1,142 days I'd been here, in my mind, thinking what was wrong with me. The voices got louder. "You can't do it," that was all that was repeating in my head. Why wouldn't it just go away? Louder and louder every second.

"Are you okay?" they asked.

"Oh yes, yes I'm fine." Little did everyone know I wasn't doing great at all. The past was just coming to me more and more every time. I was on the edge of bursting into tears. My mind was playing games. I give up... I'm lost in my mind.

Mujtaba Kazmi (13)
St Edmund's Catholic Academy, Wolverhampton

The Darkness

With a startled gasp Kian awoke, yet he saw nothing other than the darkness enveloping his system. He tugged and pulled at the latches of rope confining him to this prison. As his heart began pulsating with fear, he wondered what he did to deserve this torment. While he struggled, he tapped slightly on a puddle of water causing a sensation of fear and dread. Off in the distance Kian heard slow footsteps approaching and longed for all this to end. However, he would not have that mercy but something much better, a thing he begged for. Freedom.

Kian Bowdler (12)
St Edmund's Catholic Academy, Wolverhampton

Trapped

I miss the old days, I miss my dolls. I've always been obsessed with them, a bit too much. When I was asleep, the dolls would always move. One day, they talked to me. They told me if I kept my mouth shut they'd help me. When I agreed, the dolls giggled. Every day I'd stay in my room. But I was slowly turning into something familiar and didn't care. My mother then checked up on me.

"Sam, what are you doing?" she shouted.

But Sam wasn't there. Well... I was. But I was one of them. I'm trapped. Help!

Pavneet Kaur
St Edmund's Catholic Academy, Wolverhampton

Stranger Street

Thunder, lightning, screams. I was plunged into pure darkness. Suddenly, a flash of light appeared and I found myself standing in a forest. I stood dazed, unsure what to think. The eerie silence made me shiver and a deadly draft of wind threw me flat onto my face. I looked up hesitantly and saw an unwelcoming house. Before I had any time to think, something was pushing me forwards... My heart pounded. I froze as a cold hand touched me...
Panting like a dog, my eyes opened and I was lying on a hospital bed, or that's what I thought.

Niamh O'Donnell (11)
St Edmund's Catholic Academy, Wolverhampton

The Kill Of Emotions

Hate, ugly, fat, disgrace. Every bad word you can think of has been said to me. It's like being trapped in a black hole and you're floating in outer space. I can't describe the pain. Just an ocean of horrible words coming closer and then *pow!* It turns into a tsunami. You try to gasp for air but keep sinking. Each time you swim up the words keep coming towards you. No matter how hard you try, you can't escape and soon it's just pitch-black. Nothing to see and nothing good to think of. Who else feels this pain?

Lara Hiwa (11)
St Edmund's Catholic Academy, Wolverhampton

The Silencer

I couldn't move. The same wooden chair. Stuck in the same room for months, however it felt like years. "I wish I could stop time so I don't have to feel the pain," I told myself every day.

"Just talk," he said with a malicious grin on his face. These words lingered in my head day in, day out. The only light in this miniature, dark hole was from underneath the door. My escape route. From the corner of my eye I saw it. Needle in his dominant hand. The time was here again. My voice would finally be gone...

Sarrinah Hussain (12)
St Edmund's Catholic Academy, Wolverhampton

Trapped

Stuck. Trapped. Afraid. I've been getting weaker every day, feeling my powers slowly fading away. The orphanage was better. I should've stayed hidden that day. I knew something that could save me and the others or leave me dead. Every day I used to stare at the dead grass, until I found some people I could trust. I trusted them enough to tell them what I knew. At first they were stunned, but after a while their memories returned. We made a plan to escape. When the day came, we fled back home where we could finally be happy.

Emmanuella Addo (12)
St Edmund's Catholic Academy, Wolverhampton

I'm Alive

"I'm alive!" she screamed, but she knew she was really never alive. Bella Hoggs was a beautiful girl who was sat being tortured inside of me. The first pile of dirt was shovelled on. The dirt became so heavy I began to sag, squishing Bella. She had tried so hard to escape her chains, sweat had invaded every part of her body. She was done. She had tried everything to escape but Alfie had got the best of her and ended her life. She carried on fighting until she could no longer move a muscle. Her eyes slowly closed.

Rose Mason (12)
St Edmund's Catholic Academy, Wolverhampton

The Elevator

My awareness of my surroundings enhanced as the walls closed in. My breathing quickened, the man behind me took a step forward. He pressed a sequence of floors and turned around and gave me an impossibly wide grin. Suddenly the elevator dropped, the floors went into negatives, the elevator lights flickered and the man was nowhere to be seen. The elevator shook and shuddered, the walls were squeezing the life out of me. My vision blurred and everything went black as I hit the ground and everything in my body snapped.

Panashe Shoniwa (13)
St Edmund's Catholic Academy, Wolverhampton

Caged

Sun beaming into my eyes, I woke up. My head ached and my under eyes were puffy. I looked around, bars everywhere. The only light coming through a small window also barred up. I tilted my head out of the barred door, only to see hundreds of kids all barred up in matchbox-sized cells, all with the same look of confusion on their faces.

Each cell was pitch-black apart from the one beam of light coming through each rusty window. I tried to remember how I got here, but even the slightest thought made my head hurt.

Grace Watkiss-Rooney (12)
St Edmund's Catholic Academy, Wolverhampton

The Lift Full Of Strange Things

The lift stopped, suddenly I was filled with fear. My heart beating with blood moving everywhere in my body. One woman screamed and fell to the ground. The lights turned off, the electricity struggling to work, the lift becoming dark. For a moment, I thought I saw a person with a burnt face, but then it was nobody. The light kept turning on and off. I thought I was going to die. I couldn't see anything. I panicked with pain and misery. Then I felt a knife in my stomach but... it was just a nightmare. I woke up.

Mohammed Toqir (13)
St Edmund's Catholic Academy, Wolverhampton

In This Fiery Place

In 100 days I sat here and thirty seconds were ticking down. I was trapped alone, feeling lonely, and around I only saw darkness. I was unsure what it was, maybe it was a dungeon or a prison. If you were here you'd spot me alone with nothing to do, just watching this place collapse.

Then I found an escape tunnel which led somewhere. So I went into it and then I saw light. I was out, not trapped, had freedom and the nightmares were over. So if you find a tunnel that leads you out, then you're safe.

Oskar Zalewczak (11)
St Edmund's Catholic Academy, Wolverhampton

Trapped

Darkness fills my eyes. My head is thumping inside my skull. I blink violently as I search around, looking for an answer. My arms... they can't move. Panic fills my body as I try to move. Where am I? Why can't I move? My heart starts to pound and I hear it in my ears. Trying to clear the fog in my head, what's the last thing I remember? I squint my eyes to concentrate. The car. The blue flashing lights. The shouting of voices. The doctors. The silence. Then it comes to me. I'm in a coffin...

Evie Neale
St Edmund's Catholic Academy, Wolverhampton

Haunted House

I'm lying in bed. I awake to my windows being opened with a gust of wind, my blinds flying up in the air. A shadow is standing by the window, you could see the shimmer in their eyes. They start to chant these strange words. Before I know it I'm standing outside. What I can only picture is a house, it looks like somebody used to live here. I enter the house. I start to look around the house. As I turn the corner into another room, there's somebody standing up in the middle of the room. Who is it?

Mia-Mae McDermott (12)
St Edmund's Catholic Academy, Wolverhampton

The Ticking Bus

Only thirty seconds left until this bus blows up. Everyone looks so scared, so terrified! We need to find a way out. The doors are locked, the windows are bulletproof, there's no way out! One by one, we watch the terrifying clock go down. 23, 22, 21... time is running out! I look around and see the terror in people's faces. The numbers are still ticking, 10, 9, 8... Everyone is crying, as we watch the devastating numbers get to the last three seconds. We wait for the end of our lives. 3, 2, 1...

Daniel Francis (12)
St Edmund's Catholic Academy, Wolverhampton

Addiction

"You could stop whenever you want to..." is what I always heard, but the monster kept on beckoning me, saying I couldn't do without. No matter what I tried, no matter what I did... I was trapped in the claws of the monster and it was eating me ever so slowly. Abandoned by the world, searching for a way out. All out of money and with debt becoming an inevitable void. I was done for... or so I thought. My friends reached out to me, pulling me free. Alcohol was no longer destroying me.

Chimeremma Agbasoga (13)
St Edmund's Catholic Academy, Wolverhampton

Dark-Minded

"Who am I? How did I get here?" A dark room with bright green lights in every corner surrounded me. "What is my name? Where do I live?" Out of the corner of my eye I detected a white door with a rusty black handle.

I shoved the door open and it let out an ominous creak as I stared at the mysterious room before me. It was darker than the last room and there was just a birch wood desk with a slip on it. I picked up the slip and instantly knew why I was in this nightmare.

Eshan Ali (12)

St Edmund's Catholic Academy, Wolverhampton

Trapped!

Trapped. No way out. I search for something, anything, a crevice, a seal, but the walls are shiny surfaces with no clues as to how I got in here in the first place. There is no door, there are no odours and the blackness is absolute not a trace of light anywhere. My prison is a perfect cube, the corners just reachable if I extend my arms like a starfish. My breathing is steady, my mind still focused. If there was a way in there is a way out, it's just a matter of thinking until I find it.

Isha Bawal
St Edmund's Catholic Academy, Wolverhampton

Forgotten Soul

"Leave if you want to..." The same eerie words rang in my head. If only it was that simple, I would have had a chance to hug my loved ones. Pitch-black, no noise and only the lurking shadows to comfort me, this was worse than hell. I was to be forgotten, if I wasn't able to escape. My eyes now adjusted to the darkness and my head deceived me, making me hallucinate. I wasn't alone, I refused to believe it. Now, water cascaded down my face and I realised death was inevitable.

Lewis Aneke (12)
St Edmund's Catholic Academy, Wolverhampton

Just Breathe

"Bye Lucy," laughed Annabelle.

"Hahaha, let me out now!" shouted Lucy, hiding her nerves. *Slam!* Was that the car door? The car engine came to life. Sweat poured out of her like a fountain. Heart, in her dry cracked throat. Silence. The walls of the closet crept nearer and nearer. The aroma of mould suffocated her. She screamed. Silence answered back, she could barely breathe. She glanced at her watch, she gasped. Her flight to go home... had just taken off.

Eleanor McHale (13)
St Edmund's Catholic Academy, Wolverhampton

Hostages

1,142 days I'd been here. It was Thursday morning, 6:30am. I woke up to the trembling voice of a very young female hostage. Was it her? I looked to the side of me to find her gone. I started to worry. I stood up and as soon as I went to-*bang!* I heard a faint scream and then a loud thud. I ran as fast as I could and I peeked through the door to find her lying there surrounded by a blood puddle.

I suddenly woke up and saw her fast asleep. It was just a nightmare, right?

Matilda Clothier (12)
St Edmund's Catholic Academy, Wolverhampton

Make Or Break

Day four, my plan was starting to come together. Yes, what I did was wrong, but it was for all the right reasons. One guard stationed at every possible exit. Impossible? No... Guard one goes on break at 11:35 then there is a two-minute gap where the next guard fills in. I need to get out or the whole plan would fail, the plan which would save lives. It was time... The guard had gone on break... One minute to remove the air vent. Done! I made it out. The murder could now be completed.

Taran Singh Bougan (13)
St Edmund's Catholic Academy, Wolverhampton

Trapped

I could feel them staring at the back of my head, whispering and laughing. I never felt so insecure. I could feel myself going red. I turned to look at the clock. It had only been three minutes since I last checked. My legs felt like jelly. My hands had gone all sweaty. My chest was getting tighter and a million thoughts were rushing through my head. I couldn't concentrate. It felt like this happened every day. I just felt trapped...

Lucy Connell (13)

St Edmund's Catholic Academy, Wolverhampton

Alone

Alone I was on a cold winter's night. My friends are still not here. I wait some more, but they are in the distance. It was Jack crawling along on his hands and knees, but for what he did to me I cannot forgive him nor help him. The scars on my face, the pain in my back. But he's in need, groaning on the empty streets. No, I must help him. Again alone on the cold winter's night.

Charlie Passmore (11)
St Edmund's Catholic Academy, Wolverhampton